C01 083 724X

RILEY THE BRAVE'S SENSATIONAL SENSES

Help for Sensory and Emotional Challenges

D1438963

Jessica Sinarski

Illustrated by Zachary Kline

Jessica Kingsley Publishers
London and Philadelphia

First published in Great Britain in 2022 by Jessica Kingsley Publishers
An imprint of Hodder & Stoughton Ltd
An Hachette Company

1

Copyright © Jessica Sinarski 2022
Illustrations copyright © Jessica Sinarski 2022

The right of Jessica Sinarski to be identified as the Author of the Work
has been asserted by her in accordance with the Copyright, Designs and
Patents Act 1988.

Front cover image source: Zachary Kline

All rights reserved. No part of this publication may be reproduced, stored in
a retrieval system, or transmitted, in any form or by any means without the
prior written permission of the publisher, nor be otherwise circulated in any
form of binding or cover other than that in which it is published and without
a similar condition being imposed on the subsequent purchaser.

A CIP catalogue record for this title is available from the British Library and
the Library of Congress

ISBN 978 1 83997 311 6
eISBN 978 1 83997 312 3

Printed and bound in China by Leo Paper Products Ltd

Jessica Kingsley Publishers' policy is to use papers that are natural,
renewable and recyclable products and made from wood grown in
sustainable forests. The logging and manufacturing processes are expected
to conform to the environmental regulations of the country of origin.

Jessica Kingsley Publishers
Carmelite House
50 Victoria Embankment
London EC47 0DZ

www.jkp.com

DUNDEE CITY
COUNCIL

LOCATION
CENTRAL CHILDREN'S

ACCESSION NUMBER
CO1 083 724 T

SUPPLIER   PRICE
ASK

CLASS No.   DATE
                  24/10/22

For Mattie.
My love, my partner in parenting and play—thank you
for all you have done to make this possible.

—JS

ANIMAL
COUNTY
FAIR

MAY 21–
MAY 28

THIS W

This is Riley the Brave and his safe big critters.

Riley has always wanted to go to the annual Animal County Fair, but every year it has ended badly.

One year, the smells were too stinky.

Another time, the flashing lights and sounds
of metal scraping were just too much.

Riley wondered how he could ever go on the fun rides at the fair when just making it to school felt overwhelming.

On the school bus...

It was hard to focus on his friends with all those sensations —the feelings inside and outside of Riley's body—constantly distracting him. Riley felt hot, frustrated, fidgety, and stressed.

Sometimes he felt so many mixed-up sensations at once that his body and brain got overwhelmed

He might have a porcupine moment, grumping at his friend Ernie...

or get stuck in a long turtle moment, not wanting to talk to anyone. Riley wondered if he could ever feel...normal (whatever that was).

SQUEAK!
SQUEAK!

loud

bumpy

achy

One afternoon, during a particularly loud, bumpy, achy, scratchy day at school, Riley had a big tiger moment. He yelled at Ms. McGarey.

Cubs are not supposed to yell at their teachers.

He spent the afternoon bus ride worried about the note Ms. McGarey sent home with him.

NOTE

Riley had a tiger moment today. I think his senses get overwhelmed at times. I recommend reaching out to Miss Lena, a therapist who helps brave students like Riley.

Ms. McGarey

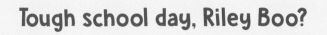

Nice to meet you. I'm Miss Lena.

Miss Lena led Riley into a big room where he soon learned he could jump, climb, swing, crash, and get squished in all the most wonderful ways. After Riley explored the room a bit, Miss Lena said,

Are you ready to learn about your sensational senses?

"Our senses give our brains lots of information," Miss Lena explained. "It gets confusing, especially because there are more than five senses. If I sway my head side to side, my sense of balance notices the movement and helps me not fall over," she said, tumbling onto the soft floor mat.

taste

smell

touch

sight

hearing

balance

proprioception

Another important sense is proh-pree-oh-SEP-shun. It helps your body feel connected to your brain.

All these senses
have to work
together for us
to feel safe, calm,
and in control.

"Think about when you are sitting on the bus," Miss Lena continued. "You see, hear, and smell a lot, but your sense of balance and all your muscles are also sending messages to your brain."

"If our senses are sending confusing signals, it is really easy to go from being a super-cool cub to having a big tiger moment."

sight

hearing

proprioception

Riley slumped onto the big cushion nearby.
"That happens to me a lot," he said glumly.
"That's exactly why we are here!" said Miss Lena, leaping over to Riley.

"Every cub—and big critter—has to get to know their own
body and brain. I have a whole list of tricks we can try."

SENSATIONAL SENSES

crunchy snack

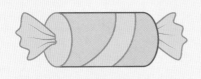
hard candy

bubblegum

straw

essential oils

scented bubbles

paw massage

towel rub

texture fun

sunglasses

visual timer

slanted desk

music

special headphones

quiet area

PROPRIOCEPTION

 squishes

 squeezes

 heavy work

 burrito bear

 heavy backpack

 trampoline

 push and pull

 wall push

 weighted blanket

 crash pad

BALANCE

 swing

 spin

 obstacle course

 wobble seat

 crawl

"Can I start with the trampoline?" asked Riley.

"Absolutely!" said Miss Lena. "So, Riley, do you think we could work together to help you make sense of your senses?"

Riley said, "If I get to keep jumping, then YES!"

Riley did keep jumping.
He jumped a lot over the next
few months. He crashed and
swung and crawled.

He rocked and rolled to build the
muscles in his belly and neck that
Miss Lena said would help him
feel less tired at school.

He pretended to be
Superbear to strengthen
his back.

It was hard work figuring out what his body needed so that he could feel calm and in control.

He got to try all kinds of new tricks, like chewing gum (loved it),

sucking sour candy (did not like it),

and taking a quiet break (liked it sometimes).

He even found that listening to his favorite song helped him eat some healthy foods he hadn't wanted to try before.

Riley tried Miss Lena's tricks on the bus too. He figured out that having his heavy backpack on his lap helped him not kick the seat in front of him. It was getting easier to join in conversations with his friends now that his senses were not feeling so overwhelmed. Lately, there had been one topic on everyone's mind: the Animal County Fair.

That afternoon, Riley asked Miss Lena,
"Do you think I'll finally have fun at the fair this year?"

"I think we can make a plan that lets you feel safe and in control," she said with a wink.

"Will I ever just feel normal?" Riley moaned.

"'Normal' is a funny word," said Miss Lena, as Riley started jumping on the trampoline.

"Not as funny as pro-pree-oh-SEP-shun," said Riley, punctuating each syllable with a big bounce.

"Ha! That's true," said Miss Lena. "I mean that I'm not sure anyone knows what 'normal' feels like. We all have to figure out what our brains and bodies need."

Riley worked hard on his **sensational plan for**

feeling safe and in control at the fair.

It was finally time to go to the Animal County Fair! Riley's first stop had to be Joey's Bounce House. Jorge was already inside. Riley didn't mind all the sounds as long as he was jumping.

"You should come to the bumper cars next," Jorge called over the noise.

Wanting to stay with his friend, Riley climbed out of the bounce house. They walked by some fried food that did not smell good as the lights flashed, and the gears grinded on all the rides around him.

The bumper cars certainly bumped! Riley tried to work the pedals, but the other cars kept jostling him in ways that did not feel safe and in control. As they got off the ride, Jorge shouted, "I see the Twist-a-Tron! And there's Ernie!"

"Here, Riley Boo," Sweets whispered in his ear, handing him a big piece of bubble gum. Riley popped it in his mouth and chewed.

Riley felt his body relax as they pushed and pulled against each other, swinging a bit as they strolled away from the crowd.

"I don't know if I can do it," Riley finally admitted.

"You don't have to." After a moment Sweets continued, "But if you want to, I think you have a **sensational plan for feeling safe and in control** that can help you get there."

Riley tucked his gum in his cheek and took three long, slow, deep breaths.

Squeezed and bounced and ready to face the Twist-a-Tron,
Riley caught up with Ernie and Jorge. He tossed a mint into
his mouth and took off his headphones.

"Where did you go?" asked Ernie.

"I just needed a minute," said Riley, smiling up at his safe big critters.
As the three friends reached the front of the line, Riley checked
in with his senses and feelings one more time.

TWIST-A-TRON

3

TICKETS

Riley was not sure if he felt normal, but it didn't matter anymore.
Riley felt **sensational!**

Afterword (for grown-ups)

Making sense of our senses

This book was written to help children (and adults) understand their sensational senses a little bit better. Our sensory systems are sending eleven million bits of information to the brain every second! Even though we are only conscious of 40–50 of those bits, it is easy to see how the brain can get flooded. When overwhelmed, the brain tends to produce some mixed-up feelings and frustrating behaviors, those "downstairs brain moments" you see in the Riley the Brave books. Here are some clues that a child might benefit from some sensory support:

- difficulty with grooming (dressing, bathing, brushing teeth and hair, cutting nails)

- constantly in motion (climbing, jumping, or crashing into things)

- difficulty moving from one activity to the next or difficulty changing plans

- easily overwhelmed, frequent meltdowns

- picky eating (extra sensitive to smells and textures, won't mix food, limited food choices)

- aggressive play

- clumsy movements, little understanding of personal space

- floppy posture, frequent slouching

- avoids play that involves getting hands wet or dirty

- highly sensitive to, or oblivious of, sights and sounds.

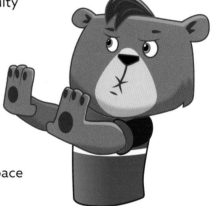

When children do not behave the way we expect them to, it is often because they *can't...* yet. Fortunately, that is not the end of the story. When we help children understand what their senses need, we create a path for social-emotional development to flourish. Read on for some strategies to better integrate our sensational senses with each other and with our powerful brains.

Why our senses matter

Early life is meant to be a sensory-rich time. Bouncing and patting a baby in your arms, snuggling in the rocking chair and singing lullabies, sucking on a binkie and being swaddled for sleep—these actions provide the diverse sensations that the infant's brain and body need.

For some families it takes more time to figure out the right combination of soothing moves to help the baby settle. Plus, it seems like as soon as you figure out something that works, it changes, forcing you to tune in to your baby's needs again and try something different to soothe your fussy little one. This process is called co-regulation. The grown-up brings their calm and curious self to help the baby with whatever is upsetting them, whether it is a wet diaper, feeling hungry or cold, or needing help falling asleep. You essentially become a sensory detective without even realizing it, and all your hard work helps that little brain and body make the foundational connections that will shape the child's future.

Sound dramatic? Maybe, but the truth is, everything we think, feel, say, and do is related to the information coming in from our senses. If you are struggling with challenging behaviors, checking in with the senses is a good place to start!

Why learn about eight senses?

You may have noticed a few more senses here than you were taught as a kid. It was a surprise to me too when I first learned about the sense of balance (also known as the vestibular system), proprioception, and interoception, which is the eighth sense. It was even more surprising to learn how vital these senses are to feeling safe and healthy in our daily lives. Here is a quick introduction to our "hidden senses."

Proprioception

Proprioception is your sense of self in space. It comes into your brain from receptors in the muscles and joints all over your body. This information lets you drink from a glass without looking and walk down a hall without touching the walls or staring at your feet (i.e. getting help from your sense of touch or sight). With its connection to the muscles and joints of the body, this sense plays a big role in planning our movements and what we often think of as "self-control." Without the right amount of proprioceptive input, it is difficult to keep your hands to yourself, write (a surprisingly complicated physical activity), climb stairs, catch a ball, or even sit still! The jumping, crashing, squishing, squeezing, pushing, and pulling that nourish this sense tend to be enjoyable and regulating for most kids.

MY SENSATIONAL SENSES

touch
- ★ Sensed by the skin all over my body
- ★ Lets me explore with my hands
- ★ Protects me from pain

smell
- ★ Teams up with taste
- ★ Protects me from stinky things
- ★ Connects with emotions and memories

hearing
- ★ Helps me enjoy music and conversation
- ★ Tunes in to danger signals
- ★ Sensitive to tone of voice

taste
- ★ Allows me to enjoy food
- ★ Helps protect me from poison

sight
- ★ Helps me plan what to do next
- ★ Alerts me to danger

balance
- ★ Notices even small head movements
- ★ Helps me feel stable and anchored
- ★ Protects me from feeling wobbly and unsafe

interoception
- ★ Senses what is happening *inside* my body, like heartbeat, breath, and OUCH that hurts
- ★ Helps me know if I am hot or cold, hungry, thirsty, or have to go potty

proprioception
- ★ Comes from my muscles and joints
- ★ Helps my body feel connected to my brain
- ★ Protects me from bumping into things

Since we have muscles and joints in our mouths, chewing gum gives the proprioceptive system a boost. When I first sought help for my sensory-seeking four-year-old son, the occupational therapist advised me to have him chew gum. The two weeks that followed were his first meltdown-free weeks ever. We needed to use a lot more of Miss Lena's tricks to help him make sense of his senses, but gum is still a trusty tool for several members of my family.

The vestibular system

This important sense begins its work in utero. Called "balance" in the story, the vestibular system is *so much more!* It is constantly detecting the head's position via tiny receptors in the inner ear. Among other things, this helps prevent brain injury by keeping the head upright. Plus, with its location so close to the brainstem and emotional center of the brain, the vestibular system is a key player in feeling safe and in control.

Healthy development requires *lots* of experiences of rocking, rolling, swinging, and crawling. Interesting sights and sounds draw the attention of babies and toddlers, nourishing their vestibular system as they move their heads to look. If your child did not have these experiences early in life, their sensational senses will need some extra support. When inviting kids into these kinds of activities, it is important to pay attention to each child's unique response. The vestibular sense is intimately linked to our sense of safety and danger. What feels just right to you might feel terrifying to your kiddo.

Interoception

While there wasn't room in the story for the eighth sensational sense, it is no less important! In fact, this sense that comes from receptors inside our body gives us lots of critical information for everyday life, like "Hey, you're hungry," and "Ow, don't touch that." It also helps us feel our emotions, like the tightness you might notice in your chest when you feel anxious or the heat up the back of your neck when you are angry. Environments and activities that help kids feel safe and in control create space for increased attention to those internal messages. Making connections out loud about your own sensations can serve as a great model for kids who might struggle with the self-reflection and mindfulness that nurture this important sense.

Sensory diet

Your sensational plan for feeling safe and in control

This is not just for the home! Educators can make small changes in the school environment that have a big impact. Building movement and big-muscle activities into your day will help you spend less time dealing with challenging behavior. This frees you up to teach and helps your students be ready to learn! A few sensory-friendly tips for the classroom:

- use gentle lighting

- reduce distracting noises (tennis balls on chair legs, fabric on walls)

- provide visual schedules

- offer flexible seating (standing, lying on the floor, wobble cushions)

- take frequent movement breaks

- incorporate proprioception activities during times of transition (wall push-ups between subjects; jump to your spot in line and then take a big, deep breath; give yourself a hug when you get back from lunch)

- engage energetic children in heavy muscle work, such as moving desks or carrying a heavy box of books to another teacher.

A quick caution with balance activities: While obstacle courses and crawling are good choices for most kids, swinging and spinning can be dysregulating for those who struggle with sensory processing. Remember, the vestibular system is tied to our sense of safety, so it is especially important that those activities never be forced on a child.

More help with sensory processing difficulties

Our senses help us enjoy life, but when they are confused or overwhelmed, they get extra protective! Sensory processing difficulties (sometimes called Sensory Processing Disorder, or SPD) impact every aspect of life. It can be confusing to detect because there are so many combinations of how our senses might be interacting with each other. If you found yourself nodding along while reading this afterword, your child may benefit from occupational therapy for sensory integration.

Children who had stressful experiences early in life, such as foster care, medical trauma, or other big disruptions, commonly struggle with sensory processing difficulties. In fact, almost everyone with a trauma history benefits from some help making sense of their sensational senses.

Perhaps as you are reading this, you are realizing that *you* could have benefited from some of Miss Lena's tricks as a child. It is never too late to make a sensational plan for feeling safe and in control! Keeping reading for additional resources for you and the brave cubs in your life.